The Diwali Nose and Other Marathi Tales

Anuradha Khati Rajivan

Rupa & Co

Published 2005 by

Rupa . Co

7/16, Ansari Road, Daryaganj,
New Delhi 110 002

Sales Centres:

Allahabad Bangalore Chandigarh Chennai
Hyderabad Jaipur Kathmandu
Kolkata Mumbai Pune

Typeset in 11.5 pts. Nalandatim by
Nikita Overseas Pvt. Ltd.
1410 Chiranjiv Tower
43 Nehru Place
New Delhi 110 019

Printed in India by
Saurabh Printers Pvt Ltd
A-16 Sector-IV
Noida 201 301

Contents

Foreword

The origin of these Marathi tales cannot really be restricted to what is today's Maharashtra, which is a political boundary. No doubt, there are variants of these stories in several languages. In selecting and retelling them I have relied on childhood memories of my grandmother's storytelling, and more recent assistance from my mother. I cannot claim to have been faithful to any 'original' version since what is original is itself not certain. The book is a collection of what I loved listening to over and over again as a child.

The stories can be read on one's own and also, with equal pleasure, read out to young children.

Anuradha Khati Rajivan

1

The Diwali Nose

There was a woman called Sukhi who lived with her husband. They were very happy together. But Sukhi had a problem. Her neighbour, Dukhi, was a woman who copied everything that Sukhi did. Not only that, Dukhi constantly eavesdropped with her ear pressed against the common wall that the two neighbours shared.

Dukhi would peep into Sukhi's window while passing by. If she saw a new pot or some new curtains, she would go and buy exactly the same things for herself. Dukhi once overheard Sukhi's husband saying to her, "I think you look pretty in this new orange sari!" Immediately Dukhi went to her husband and said, "See, Sukhi's husband has got her an orange sari. I want one too! And I want it today!" What a fuss she made when her husband said, "But you look much better in blue!" Finally her husband had to buy the orange sari. But Dukhi never wore it as she did not really like orange all that much! Dukhi was never happy.

Thus the days went by. Diwali was coming close. People were busy shopping. While everyone else was in a happy mood, it was a difficult time for Dukhi. She had a hard time trying to keep track of the new things Sukhi was buying. This made Sukhi uncomfortable. So she said to her husband, "Dukhi is becoming an impossible copycat. She needs to be cured of this habit."

"Yes," agreed her husband. "Her behaviour is getting worse. Let's teach her a lesson."

So Sukhi and her husband made a plan. They had to discuss the matter in very low whispers, lest Dukhi overheard anything. Then, as planned, they started talking very loudly, knowing Dukhi was at home.

Sukhi said to her husband in a loud voice, "This Diwali I want a really nice nose. Please cut it carefully on both sides."

"How about a nice cut here, and a little cut there?" asked her husband, equally loudly.

Sukhi: Use this knife, it's sharper.

Husband: Now look in the mirror. Do you like it?

Sukhi: A little bit more on the left side. Hmm. Yes.

Husband: It's perfect! In a week it will grow back to its normal size. You are going to have the prettiest nose in the neighbourhood!

Sukhi: Now put the bandage on. I want it to heal well before Diwali.

Husband: There, it's all done.

Dukhi was stunned! Did she hear right? Just to make sure, she decided to go to Sukhi's house. So, pretending that she

wanted a little curd, she went to see Sukhi. Sure enough there was a bandage on Sukhi's nose.

"What have you done to yourself?" asked Dukhi.

"Oh, it's just a small operation for my new Diwali nose," replied Sukhi.

"Diwali nose?"

"Yes, every year my husband cuts my nose and gives it a nice new shape. It grows in a week's time. This time he's done a really neat job! I'm going to look very pretty!" explained Sukhi.

Dukhi ran home at once. She was convinced that all she had heard was true. She asked her husband to cut her nose. Her husband was shocked and refused. But Dukhi made a fuss. "I want a nice new nose for Diwali. Why don't you cooperate. Sukhi's husband does it for her every year! She's really going to look pretty!"

Finally Dukhi's husband got tired of arguing. He began to cut her nose. She cried out in pain. "Should I stop?" asked her husband, alarmed.

"Of course not! If Sukhi can do it, so can I!" Dukhi replied.

So Dukhi's nose was cut and bandaged. She was in a lot of pain, but tried not to show it. That was when Sukhi took off her bandage. Dukhi saw her walking about with her usual nose. At last Dukhi understood what had happened and how foolish she had been.

From that very day, Dukhi finally stopped copying her neighbour.

$$\frac{2}{}$$

Brain Versus Brawn

In a certain town there lived two thieves. One was called Chor. He was large and strong as well as a trained wrestler. The other, called Maha Chor, was short, thin and rather frail looking. Chor was jealous that the other thief was called Maha Chor even though he was the stronger one.

One day Chor and Maha Chor met as they were both going to the neighbouring town of Karad to try and steal something. "Why don't we travel together?" Chor asked. "Sure! It will help us pass the time!" replied Maha Chor.

At Karad, Maha Chor stole a lot of money and jewels from the house of a rich merchant. Chor was less successful elsewhere, but he also completed his day's business. Both were ready to rest for the day. They took a room together for the night in a wayside place for travellers.

Chor had been eyeing Maha Chor's bulging cloth bag. "He seems to have got a huge loot! I'll steal it when he sleeps tonight!" thought Chor. He chatted very pleasantly to Maha

Chor, hoping to lower the latter's guard. After a good meal they stretched out and lay down to sleep.

Actually Chor was only pretending to sleep. He was watching Maha Chor out of the corner of his eyes. Maha Chor had used his cloth bag as a pillow. That is what Chor wanted to get his hands on. Once he was convinced that Maha Chor was fast asleep, slowly and very carefully he started searching among Maha Chor's things. But even after half an hour of careful examination he found nothing. The cloth bag only had some clothes. He searched under the bed, in Maha Chor's pockets, everywhere among his things, but in vain. "Where could this Maha Chor have hidden his loot?" wondered Chor. He couldn't get a wink of sleep the whole night!

The next two days the same thing was repeated. Both would retire for the night, Chor would only pretend to sleep and then search all of Maha Chor's belongings. But poor Chor could not lay his hands on anything in spite of spending three sleepless nights. It made Chor completely fed up and frustrated, especially as he saw Maha Chor enjoying a very peaceful sleep every night!

Finally Chor could take it no longer. He decided to ask Maha Chor outright. "Today is the last day at Karad. We return to our town. But before we get back, I want to ask you a question. Will you promise me an honest answer?" Maha Chor agreed.

"Where do you hide your loot every night? I admit I searched among your things to rob you. But how come I was not able to find anything?" Chor asked.

Do you know what Maha Chor's reply was? This is what he said: "Well, since you are a thief just like me, naturally I had to be extra careful. So each night without your realising it, I would keep my loot among your things under your bedding! You searched all my things. But you did not search for my loot among your own things! At daybreak I would put the loot back in my bag! What could be safer?"

Chor had to admit that Maha Chor was the superior of the two! "I bow to your superior brains!" Chor said, conceding that Maha Chor had a right to his name.

3

Two Travellers

Two men, Pendya and Gondya, set out to travel from their villages to the town of Wardha. On the way, they happened to meet each other at Charur village where they had stopped for some rest. Pendya was a bit of a simpleton. Gondya was a very cunning fellow and a smart talker. They soon got talking and found that both of them were going to Wardha.

"Why don't we travel together the rest of the way?" suggested Gondya.

"Good idea! Then we can chat on the way and keep each other company!" agreed Pendya.

"What's in the bundle that you're carrying?" asked Gondya.

"Oh, some sattu to eat on the way," replied Pendya. "It is made of many grains, roasted and ground. I add some sugar from this other packet, mix it with water and eat it. Sometimes, if I find milk, I add the milk instead of water. Then it tastes even better!"

"Well, I'm carrying some paddy with me. I can cook rice with it. Very soft and fluffy! Much better than sattu!" said Gondya.

Now Gondya knew that it was not so easy to cook rice starting from paddy. You first had to beat and pound the paddy to remove the tough, brown husk. Then you had to blow the husk away to get the clean grains. All this needed proper equipment. You also needed a good pot to wash and soak the rice in plenty of water before cooking. And, of course, you could go no further without a fire. The water took time to boil. The rice took time to cook. What a lot of time and effort was called for! Gondya realised that mixing sattu was far, far easier.

Cunning Gondya thought to himself, "I'm beginning to get hungry. I have to trick this foolish Pendya into giving me his sattu! If I can make him want my paddy badly, I could exchange it for his sattu. Then I'll finish it up before he has any time to change his mind!"

As he was thinking these thoughts, an idea struck him. He said to Pendya:

"Sattu's good, may well be true;
But imagine eating what looks like glue!
First you need some milk or water;
Mix and stir with lots of sugar.
All that work – your face could turn blue!"

Poor Pendya! He began to wonder if his sattu was any good at all! His face looked uncertain. Gondya realised that his trick was beginning to work. He wanted to press his advantage to make sure the foolish Pendya willingly exchanged his sattu for the paddy. So Gondya started off about his paddy:

"Easy paddy!
Beat it, then eat it!"

This made Pendya feel even worse! He thought, "I wonder if Gondya will be kind enough to exchange my sattu for his paddy? I guess I have to muster up courage to ask."

Gondya repeated the rhymes once more. Pendya could control himself no more. He said, "Please good Gondya! Will you exchange my sattu for your paddy? I've been eating sattu for so long! I'd really like a change!"

Gondya was delighted that his trick had worked! But he pretended to be a little reluctant. "Well, I'm not sure! Rice is really delicious! I don't know what your sattu tastes like!"

"Oh, but it's very tasty! It's just that I've been eating it every day!" pleaded silly Pendya, thinking that he was being rather smart.

Clever Gondya agreed. "Oh, alright!" he said. "Since you've pleaded so much, let's exchange!"

So Pendya and Gondya made the exchange. By now Gondya was very hungry. Pendya was thirsty, and not yet hungry. They stopped near a well. Gondya drew some water from the well, mixed the sattu and sugar and had a good meal! "Uuh-ba!" he burped, satisfied when all the sattu was finished. Pendya had a drink of water and the two travellers were on their way to Wardha once again.

After a while Pendya was hungry. He opened the bundle of paddy. "How do I pound it?" he asked Gondya. "You need to find a mortar and pestle to pound it with," replied Gondya. But there was no mortar and pestle around! After walking for many miles a kind woman from a wayside village agreed to let Pendya use her mortar and pestle. The chaff was removed from the grain. But it was all mixed together!

"I need a winnow to separate the chaff and the grain! I can't possibly be picking each grain out one by one!" But there was nothing to winnow with. After trudging along some more they finally found another village where a young man helped Pendya winnow his grain. The chaff was blown away. The clean grains of rice looked very nice. But Pendya could not possibly eat them raw! He now began to understand the clever trick that Gondya had played on him! But it was too late! The sattu was all eaten up! There was no way Pendya could get it back!

After walking some more the two travellers were finally nearing Wardha. Pendya had become very hungry and tired. Gondya, however, was enjoying the walk. Just as poor Pendya was about to give up and collapse, a kind woman saw the two travellers. She noticed that Pendya was in a bad shape. As her home was nearby, she invited them home. There she lit a fire and cooked the rice in a pot while Pendya rested. But plain rice! Pendya did not have anything to go with the rice! Neither did Gondya! So she offered them some curd and pickle to eat with the rice. After a long hard struggle Pendya was finally able to eat. Gondya too joined in the meal and ate heartily!

Didn't Pendya feel cheated! But it was his own doing. After all, it was he who had begged Gondya for the exchange!

Moral: Have confidence in what is yours. Do not look down upon what you have just because of another's remarks.

4

Clever Mhatari

Once upon a time there was an old woman who lived at the edge of a forest. Her name was Mhatari. She had a daughter who lived in a village on the other side of the forest. One day, Mhatari set out to visit her daughter. She packed some parathas and pickle to eat on the way.

While she was walking she met a sly fox. The fox said to her:

> "Mhatari, O Mhatari,
> I'm going to eat you up!"

The old woman replied:

> "I'm too skinny, but if you must,
> Let me go to my daughter's first.
> Eat chapatis with ghee that's precious,
> It's bound to make me plump and delicious.
> Then you may eat me up!"

The sly fox said, "Well, all right. But don't forget! I'm going to eat you up on your way back!"

The old woman walked on After a while she met a hungry wolf. The wolf barked at her:

> "Mhatari, O Mhatari,
> I'm going to eat you up!"

The old woman replied:

> "I'm too skinny, but if you must,
> Let me go to my daughter's first.
> Eat chapatis with ghee that's precious,
> It's bound to make me plump and delicious.
> Then you may eat me up!"

The hungry wolf said, "Well, all right. But don't forget! I'm going to eat you up on your way back!"

Mhatari trudged along through the forest. Then she met a ferocious bear. The bear rumbled at her:

> "Mhatari, O Mhatari,
> I'm going to eat you up!"

The old woman replied:

> "I'm too skinny, but if you must,
> Let me go to my daughter's first.
> Eat chapatis with ghee that's precious,
> It's bound to make me plump and delicious.
> Then you may eat me up!"

The ferocious bear replied, "Well, all right. But don't forget! I'm going to eat you up on your way back!"

Mhatari walked on. The forest was getting denser. On the way she met a mighty tiger. The tiger looked sharply at her and said:

> "Mhatari, O Mhatari,
> I'm going to eat you up!"

The old woman replied:

> "I'm too skinny, but if you must,
> Let me go to my daughter's first.
> Eat chapatis with ghee that's precious,
> It's bound to make me plump and delicious.
> Then you may eat me up!"

The mighty tiger replied, "Well, all right. But don't forget! I'm going to eat you up on your way back!"

Mhatari continued her journey. This time she met a majestic lion. The lion roared loudly at her:

> "Mhatari, O Mhatari,
> I'm going to eat you up!"

The old woman replied:

> "I'm too skinny, but if you must,
> Let me go to my daughter's first.
> Eat chapatis with ghee that's precious,
> It's bound to make me plump and delicious.
> Then you may eat me up!"

The majestic lion replied, "Well, all right. But don't forget! I'm going to eat you up on your way back!"

By this time Mhatari had reached the end of the forest. She crossed a clearing, a wooden bridge across a bubbling stream and finally reached her daughter's house. The daughter was delighted to see her mother.

"Welcome Ma!" the daughter said. "I hope you're not planning to return in a hurry. Do stay with me for some time."

Mhatari and her daughter spent many pleasant days together. They ate, relaxed, shared the household work, talked and caught up on old family stories. Old Mhatari even put on some weight and didn't look so skinny any more. One day Mhatari said to her daughter, "I've stayed with you for a month. It is now proper for me to return. I've had a really good time with you."

"Oh do stay longer!" pleaded her daughter. But the old woman was serious about going back. She started making preparations for her journey.

Mhatari asked her daughter to bring the largest pumpkin she could find. The daughter got a really large and orange and round pumpkin. Mhatari hollowed out the insides of the pumpkin. She also cut out a square bit from one side and fixed a door there. Next she made five packets of chilly powder. Now with preparations for her journey complete, old Mhatari was ready to return.

She opened the door of the pumpkin and settled inside it. The packets of chilly powder were with her of course. Mhatari ordered the pumpkin:

"Move on O pumpkin,
Tunuk-tunuk-tin!"

The pumpkin started rolling forward. Mhatari was on her way back in the pumpkin. She crossed the bridge across the bubbling river and the clearing. Then she entered the forest.

This time it was the majestic lion who stopped her first. "Hold it old Mhatari! Have you forgotten your promise? I've been waiting to eat you!" he roared.

Mhatari replied, "I'm ready, oh majestic lion! Just help me with the door and then you may eat me up!"

So the lion helped her open the pumpkin's door. Just as the door was half open, the old woman popped the first packet of chilly powder into the lion's eyes and quickly shut the door again.

"Ooo-eee! Ooo-eee!" yelled the lion in pain. He ran away rubbing his eyes, not looking majestic at all!

"Move on O pumpkin,
Tunuk-tunuk-tin!"

ordered old Mhatari. The pumpkin rolled along with her inside.

Next she met the mighty tiger. "Hold it O Mhatari! Have you forgotten your promise? I've been waiting to eat you!" growled the tiger.

Mhatari replied, "I'm ready, oh mighty tiger! Just help me with the door and then you may eat me up."

So the tiger helped her open the pumpkin's door. Just as the door was half open the old woman popped the second packet of chilly powder into the mighty tiger's eyes and quickly shut the door again.

"Ooo-eee! Ooo-eee!" yelled the tiger in pain, not feeling mighty at all! He ran away rubbing his eyes!

> "Move on O pumpkin,
> Tunuk-tunuk-tin!"

ordered old Mhatari as she moved on.

Next she met the ferocious bear. "Hold it O Mhatari! Have you forgotten your promise? I've been waiting to eat you!" rumbled the ferocious bear.

Mhatari replied, "I'm ready, oh ferocious bear! Just help me with the door and then you may eat me up."

So the bear helped her open the pumpkin's door. Just as the door was half open the old woman popped the third packet of chilly powder into the eyes of the ferocious bear and quickly shut the door again!

"Ooo-eee! Ooo-eee!" yelled the bear in pain, not looking ferocious at all! He ran away rubbing his eyes!

> "Move on O pumpkin,
> Tunuk-tunuk-tin!"

ordered old Mhatari and rolled on ahead.

Next she met the hungry wolf. "Hold it O Mhatari! Have you forgotten your promise? I've been waiting to eat you!" barked the wolf.

Mhatari replied, "I'm ready, oh hungry wolf! Just help me with the door and then you may eat me up."

So the hungry wolf helped her open the pumpkin's door. Just as the door was half open the old woman popped the fourth packet of chilly powder into the eyes of the wolf and quickly shut the door again!

"Ooo-eee! Ooo-eee!" yelled the wolf in pain, not feeling hungry any more! He ran away rubbing his eyes!

"Move on O pumpkin,
Tunuk-tunuk-tin!"

ordered old Mhatari, rolling along.

Finally the old woman met the sly fox. "Hold it O Mhatari! Have you forgotten your promise? I've been waiting to eat you!" said the fox. Mhatari replied, "I'm ready, oh sly fox! Just help me with the door and then you may eat me up."

So the sly fox helped her open the pumpkin's door. Just as the door was half open, the old woman popped the fifth packet of chilly powder into the eyes of the fox and quickly shut the door again!

"Ooo-eee! Ooo-eee!" yelled the fox in pain, forgetting how to be sly altogether! He ran away rubbing his eyes!

"Move on O pumpkin,
Tunuk-tunuk-tin!"

ordered the old woman.

Clever Mhatari reached home safe and sound. She had outsmarted all those who had tried to bother her.

Since then, Mhatari would sing happily:

> "Even though you're old,
> Rather weak and thin;
> A good brain conquers all,
> Tunuk-tunuk-tin!"

5

Mhatari's Berries

Old Mhatari was a clever woman. She lived in a house with a large berry tree. Every year, in season, the tree bore fat, juicy, green berries which soon ripened to a delicious red-brown. Mhatari's berries were in great demand in the neighbourhood. Every year, when the berries were ripe, she picked them and took them to the market to sell them. During the day Mhatari tended her berry tree. When the berries began to ripen she kept a close watch all day from her kitchen window to make sure no one stole the berries.

One day Kolhaa, the sly fox, was passing by. He saw the berry tree laden with fruits. The rains had been good that season and the branches were heavy with ripening berries. His mouth began to water. He was strongly tempted to taste some. "Why does an old woman need so many berries? I'm sure she won't find out if I eat just a few!" thought Kolhaa. But he noticed that the old woman was keeping a watch from her kitchen window. So he decided to try his luck at night.

Very quietly, in the dead of the night, the fox entered Mhatari's compound. It was a moon-less night and it was very dark. No one was around. "Seems like a good time to sample the ripening berries!" thought Kolhaa. He went to the berry tree and stopped. He had no intention of getting caught. So he first looked to his right and then to his left. Then he looked behind him and in front. He couldn't see anyone. "Good! I'm safe!" Kolhaa thought. Then he began to eat the juicy red berries.

"Mmm! Delicious!" he said after he had eaten a few. "No wonder the old woman guards her tree so carefully! These are absolutely the best berries I've eaten!" And Kolhaa ate some more. He kept eating until nearly half the berries on the tree were gone! By then it was dawn. An orange sun began to peep out of the horizon. "That's enough for one night!" thought Kolhaa and he ran away quickly.

After a while old Mhatari woke up. She washed and tidied herself and then went to the kitchen. She began to light the fire to start her cooking for the day. "In just a couple of days the berries will be ripe for picking. I should get a good price for them!" she thought to herself and looked out of her kitchen window. What a shock she got! She could hardly believe what she saw! Half the berries were gone! "But they were there all day yesterday! Some one has stolen them at night!" Mhatari thought, dismayed.

But being a clever old woman, Mhatari did not give up. She knew that she was smarter than most policemen. "I'll keep a watch tonight and teach the thief a lesson. He's bound to come back for more, the greedy who-ever-it-is!" she hissed to herself.

Mhatari spent her morning as usual. But in the afternoon she took a good nap. This time she was going to keep watch at night. She did not want to be too sleepy for the task. When it began to get dark, she had an early dinner of dal, rice, brinjal bharta and rotis. Then she finished washing up all the pots and pans – all except the tawa, which was still hot from making the rotis. She let the tawa sit on a low fire. Very soon it became red hot.

Mhatari turned off all the lamps in her house. It was very dark outside too. The red hot tawa began to glow in the dark. Mhatari picked up the tawa with a pair of tongs and tiptoed to her berry tree. She placed the tawa firmly among the tree's branches and slipped back into her kitchen. She found a cozy spot near the kitchen window from where she could keep a watch on the proceedings.

Sure enough, as Mhatari had expected, Kolhaa-the-fox was back that night. Greed and the previous night's easy success had prompted him to try stealing berries again. "Last night I had to leave behind the not-so-ripe berries. They must be ready tonight!" he said to himself as he crept into Mhatari's compound once again. He was more confident and less careful this time. He walked straight to the berry tree without even trying to hide.

"So Mr Kolhobaa, you're the thief!" thought Mhatari as she saw Kolhaa from her kitchen window. "You sure deserve to be punished." For the old woman had heard rumours that

Kolhaa-the-fox had been suspected of stealing hens and rabbits also. But unfortunately no one in the neighbourhood had been able to catch him red-handed so far.

Kolhaa climbed the berry tree and began eating the ripe berries. "They're even better than yesterday's! A day's wait has ripened them to perfection!" he thought, licking his lips. Very soon he saw the red hot tawa. "What is this?" he wondered. "It looks so beautiful and perfectly round! It must be a seat! Perhaps Mhatari uses it to sit while picking berries from the branches! I must give it a try!"

And so Kolhaa sat on the hot tawa! He fell off the tree at once, squealing loudly! "Ooee! Ooee!" he wailed. The fur on his bottom was singed right away and his skin there felt like it was on fire! Mhatari laughed to herself as she saw Kolhaa run away with his tail between his hind legs!

The next morning Mhatari saw Kolhaa walk down the road in the market. She could not resist calling out to him:

"Kolhobaa, O Kolhobaa!
My berries are ripe!"

Kolhaa replied:

"Oh, no, old Mhatari
Please do be a dear;
Don't tell anyone that
My bottom's on fire!"

And to this day Kolhaa-the-fox has never again tried to steal any thing.

6

Puran Poli

Old Mhatari was travelling to the town. On the way she met a young man named Madhav. Mhatari and Madhav struck up a conversation. She liked young Madhav. "You remind me of my son," Mhatari said. Madhav was pleased, especially because he did not have a mother.

After a while Madhav said, "Mhatari, I'm hungry. I have a dozen bananas. Would you like to share some with me?"

"I'm carrying some puran polis. Do you like sweet stuff? Why don't we eat them first? We can have the bananas later," Mhatari suggested.

"Sure!" agreed Madhav. "I love anything sweet! But I've never eaten a puran poli before! What's it like?" he asked.

Mhatari opened her bundle. She showed Madhav the polis and gave him one to try. Puran poli is nothing but a roti with soft, sweet and yellow channa dal stuffing inside. Mhatari had also spread a generous quantity of ghee on the outside for an even better flavour. Madhav chewed off a bit. It was delicious!

In no time at all Madhav's puran poli was finished. Mhatari also ate one. Madhav looked at old Mhatari's bundle longingly. He obviously wanted another one. Mhatari understood.

"Have some more, son. I have plenty of them in my bundle!" she said.

Madhav could not resist the offer. He took another one. He peeled off the top layer and ate it. Then he finished up the sweet stuffing inside. Finally he ate up the bottom layer. All the time he was examining each bit. He seemed quite puzzled by what he saw. It tasted very, very good. But there was something he could not understand. So he took another one. He examined it from all sides and then ate it up. After that he ate another one. And another. And yet another!

Finally he had had enough. "They were simply delicious!" said Madhav rubbing his stomach. "But Mhatari, I'm quite puzzled. There is no hole in the puran poli." Mhatari did not understand what was bothering Madhav. So he explained:

"Skin on top and skin below
In between it's sweet and yellow.
How do you stuff it all the way
Then pull your hand out anyway?"

How did Mhatari put the stuffing inside and pull her hands out without making a hole in the poli, Madhav wondered. Mhatari laughed. This is what she said:

"Take some dough and make a hollow
Fill in the stuffing sweet and yellow.

Roll it, then cook it, soft and mellow
Get the point, you silly fellow?"

Madhav understood at last! Wasn't he a silly fellow?

7

The Crow and Sparrow

There once was a crow and a sparrow. The crow lived in a house made of bits of straw bound with cow dung. The sparrow lived in a house lined with wax. One day it rained very hard. The crow's house crumbled and the bits of straw flowed away in the rain. The sparrow's house remained firm and dry.

The crow came to the sparrow's house. He knocked at the door and said:

> "Sister sparrow! Sister sparrow! Please, O please open the door!"
> The sparrow replied, "Get off you cocky crow! I'm giving my baby a bath!"

So the crow waited for a while. Then he knocked again.
> "Sister sparrow! Sister sparrow! Please, O please open the door!"
> The sparrow replied, "Get off you cocky crow! I'm powdering my baby!"

So the crow waited for a while. Then he knocked again.

"Sister sparrow! Sister sparrow! Please, O please open the door!"
The sparrow replied, "Get off you cocky crow! I'm dressing my baby!"

So the crow waited for a while. Then he knocked again.

"Sister sparrow! Sister sparrow! Please, O please open the door!"
The sparrow replied, "Get off you cocky crow! I'm feeding my baby!"

So the crow waited for a while. Then he knocked again.

"Sister sparrow! Sister sparrow! Please, O please open the door!"
The sparrow replied, "Get off you cocky crow! I'm putting my baby to sleep!"

So the crow waited for a while. Then he knocked again.

"Sister sparrow! Sister sparrow! Please, O please open the door!"

This time the sparrow opened her door. The crow came in to the clean and dry home. He was wet and shivering. The sparrow felt sorry for the crow. She asked him to sit in the warm kitchen. "There is some soft khichdi cooking in the pot. I need to go fetch some water. When I get back you can share my meal. Meanwhile, could you please stir the pot now and then?" she asked.

The crow nodded. He stood next to the fire and stirred the pot. He felt warm and cozy. The khichdi was soon done. It smelt great! It looked wonderful! The crow could not resist. He was tired and hungry.

"I'll taste just a little bit. Sparrow will never know," he thought.

So he took a spoon and scooped out a small helping. Mmmm! It was simply delicious!

"Just one more spoon! A teeny-tiny bit," he thought, helping himself. This went on and on and on ... until the khichdi was all gone!

The crow panicked. What was he to do? The sparrow had been so good to him and he had gobbled up all her food! He could not stay and face her. Just as he was wondering what to do, he heard the door rattle.

"My goodness! It's sister sparrow!" he whispered. The crow quickly opened the lid of the rice tin in the kitchen and hid inside.

Sure enough it was the sparrow. She was back with a heavy pot of water. She put down the pot and looked around. Where was the crow? He was nowhere to be seen. The sparrow went to the fire to check on the khichdi. What a shock she got to see that the pot was empty! How annoyed she became! Now she began a serious hunt for the crow. She searched under the bed and on the shelves. She looked everywhere. But there was no sign of the crow. "He must have left," she thought angrily, "after eating up all my khichdi!"

Poor sparrow! She was very hungry after all her work. "I'll just have to make some more," she grumbled as she opened the tin of rice. She felt something wet and squishy in there with the rice. Surprised, she pulled out her hand and saw that it was the crow all soggy and messy! She shook him out of the tin in anger and chased him round and round and beat him with a stick until he cried "Caw! Caw! I'm sorry sister sparrow!" And then he flew away.

8

The Strange Dependence

Part I

There once lived an old woman with her young and simple daughter-in-law. The old woman called her Soon-bai. Soon-bai called the old woman Saasu-bai. They were very happy together. The old woman taught young Soon-bai how to cook, keep a neat and tidy house, tend the farm lands and cows. Soon-bai learnt to rely on her mother-in-law for everything she did. In fact she would not do anything without first consulting the old woman.

In the morning, after waking up, Soon-bai would ask the old woman, "Saasu-bai, Saasu-bai, what should I do?"

The old woman would reply, "Brush your teeth." And the daughter-in-law would brush her teeth.

Then Soon-bai would ask, "Saasu-bai, Saasu-bai, should I clean the porch?"

The old woman would reply, "Yes, do." Then the daughter-in-law would clean the porch.

Soon-bai would ask, "Saasu-bai, Saasu-bai, should I take a bath?"

The old woman would reply, "Hurry up, do." Then the daughter-in-law would go for her bath.

Soon-bai would ask, "Saasu-bai, Saasu-bai, what vegetable should we cook today?" The old woman would reply, "Let's make some beans." And so they would sit down, cut and cook the beans for their morning meal.

Soon-bai would ask, "Saasu-bai, Saasu-bai, should I make some rice?"

The old woman would reply, "Yes, do." Then the daughter-in-law would make some rice.

When harvest time came the daughter-in-law would ask, "Saasu-bai, Saasu-bai, should we go to the fields?"

The old woman would reply, "Yes! There's a lot of work to be done." The two of them would pack some food and set out to work.

The old woman and her young daughter-in-law carried on like this for many years. All the work at home and in the fields got done. Their store was always full of grain. The home was neat and tidy. The family was contented. Young Soon-bai's husband did not even know about this unusual dependence of his wife.

Eventually the old woman died. Soon-bai lost her Saasu-bai. Whom was she to consult from now on? She could not get any work done at home or in the fields. The place began

to look dirty. Soon-bai began to look sloppy. Food was not cooked. The cows were not milked on time. The fields were neglected. Nothing seemed to work. The husband began to get impatient with her.

Soon-bai realised that something had to be done. So she made a rag doll as a substitute for her mother-in-law. She dressed the doll in a strip of her mother-in-law's sari and placed it in a corner of her home.

Every morning she would ask the rag doll, "Saasu-bai, Saasu-bai, should I brush my teeth?"

Then she herself would answer, "Yes," and pretend that her old mother-in-law had said so. Only after that would she go and brush her teeth.

She would then ask the doll, "Saasu-bai, Saasu-bai, should I clean the porch?" Again pretending that the mother-in-law had said yes, Soon-bai would clean the porch.

In this way all the work began to get done once again. The home began to look clean. The fields were tended. Soon-bai herself started looking neat and tidy once more.

It was not as if Soon-bai was good-for-nothing. The problem was in her mind. Often the mind can be very powerful indeed. The rag doll seemed to have solved the problem neatly. But did it really?

9

Soon-Bai and Rukma-Bai

Part II

Soon-bai's husband did not like the idea that his wife constantly talked to a doll. Every time he wanted to talk to her about something, he would find her in the corner consulting the rag doll. It began to get on his nerves. He thought his wife was going crazy. One day he said to himself, "If I continue to live with this woman I'm bound to go crazy myself."

When he could stand it no longer, he chased poor Soon-bai out of the house. "Get lost, woman! And don't come back!" he shouted. Soon-bai was a simple woman. She was used to obeying others because of her unusual relationship with her mother-in-law. So she picked up the rag doll and left the house without any complaint.

She walked many miles and soon reached the edge of a forest. It was getting dark. She began to worry that some wild animal would attack her. So Soon-bai asked the rag doll, "I'm scared, Saasu-bai. It's so dark. Should I climb up this tree? It's likely to be safer than sleeping on the ground!"

Then Soon-bai climbed up the tree with her doll. After a while she heard voices from below. It seemed as if some men were talking in hushed voices. She peeped down from above. A gang of robbers had assembled under that tree. They were putting all their loot together and sharing out whatever they had stolen that day. Soon-bai became even more frightened. She started trembling and dropped the rag doll. It fell right in the middle of the loot that the gang was dividing!

Now, robbers are very often superstitious and believe in spirits and ghosts. They were terrified to see the rag doll fall from the sky! They did not know what it was and began to shout in panic.

"What on earth can it be! It's probably some ghost!" said the head robber, quite scared. "We'd better hurry away before something terrible happens!" said another.

The gang of robbers ran away, leaving all their loot behind. Soon-bai climbed down the tree in the morning. She saw the gold and the piles of money that the robbers had left there. She picked up everything, tied it up in the pallu of her sari and started back home.

When she reached home, Soon-bai knocked at the door of her house and called out to her husband:

"Open the door, do please hurry up!
I'm loaded, and can hardly stand up!"

Her husband was quite surprised to see Soon-bai with so much wealth. He had thought that she was crazy and good-for-nothing. Now she had proved him wrong. He was very pleased to have her back. "She may be odd, but she sure has brought me good luck!" he thought to himself.

Soon-bai was happy to be back home. Being a simple woman, she wanted to share her happy story with her neighbour, Rukma-bai. So Soon-bai told Rukma-bai, the whole story.

Now Rukma-bai was a greedy woman. No one liked her because of this. She thought, "I should do what this foolish woman did. Then I'll become rich and my husband will begin to love me."

So Rukma-bai also made a rag doll for herself. She asked her husband to chase her out of the house. Then she went to the forest and climbed up the same tree. Sure enough, at night, the gang of robbers assembled under the tree. Rukma-bai threw down the doll.

Now, the head robber was a smart man, even though he was superstitious. This time he began to get suspicious. "Dolls can't be falling down again and again. Wait everybody! We must investigate!" he declared.

"Yes! This is happening once too often!" agreed another robber.

So two men climbed up the tree. They found the greedy Rukma-bai and dragged her down. "Leave me alone! Please let me go!" she pleaded.

"So, you were the one who pinched all our loot the last time!" said the head robber angrily.

"It wasn't me! It was my neighbour!" Rukma-bai tried to explain.

But naturally no one believed her. They thought she was greedy, which she was; and a liar, which she was not. Anyway, the robbers were so angry with her that they cut off her nose and sent her packing. Poor Rukma-bai! She had learnt her lesson. She ran all the way home, knocked at the door and called out to her husband:

> "Open the door, do hurry up!
> I'm bleeding, my nose is cut up!"

10

The Rat Who Married the Princess

Once a rat found a nail cutter from the roadside. 'How do I use it?' he wondered. 'All decent people look after their nails. I'd like to clean and trim mine too!' he said to himself. But try as he might, he could not use the nail cutter.

So the rat went to the barber. 'Here is my nail cutter. Could you please trim my nails for me?' the rat asked.

The barber found such a request rather funny. 'Why not humour him?' he thought. So he agreed to trim the rat's nails. But the rat's nails were hard. As the barber was trimming them, the nail cutter broke.

'You broke my nice nail cutter! You broke my nail cutter!' wailed the rat. 'Either you return my nail cutter as it was, or you give me your scissors!' he demanded, creating quite a scene at the barber's shop. The barber did not want any trouble in front of his customers so he gave the rat a pair of scissors and was glad to see the last of him.

The rat took his newly-acquired pair of scissors and scampered off. He saw a cloth shop and entered it. The shopkeeper was intrigued to see such a sight. 'What do you want?' he asked the rat. 'I want some thick cloth to make a strong bag,' replied the rat. 'And you can take these scissors of mine in exchange.'

'Here is some really strong fabric,' replied the shopkeeper. 'Hand me your scissors and I will cut it for you.'

But when the shop keeper began to cut the cloth, the scissors broke! 'You broke my new pair of scissors!' complained the rat. 'Either you return it as it was, or give me some cloth in exchange!' So saying the rat jumped up and down and threw quite a tantrum. To avoid any more fuss, the shopkeeper gave the rat a yard of some really soft and silky fabric. 'Here, take this. Notice its pearly sheen. The fabric is so soft, it is fit for the princess!' said the shopkeeper, wanting to get rid of the rat as fast as possible.

The rat took the soft fabric and ran to find a tailor. The idea of meeting the princess began to take shape in his mind. 'Why not? Why can't a rat meet the princess?' he thought, running in the direction of the palace. 'But first I need some clothes. It may not be proper to meet the princess with nothing on!'

On the way to the palace lived a tailor. The rat went to the tailor's house and showed the tailor his fabric. 'Can you make a nice shirt out of this cloth for me?' he asked.

The tailor handled the soft and silky cloth that the rat had brought in. As he was feeling the cloth and admiring its pearly sheen, he thought of how nice a blouse in this fabric would look on his wife when she wore her pearl jewelry. He had brought her pearl ring with him to get it cleaned and polished and he put the ring against the cloth to see how they looked together. Now, the tailor loved his wife very much, but she had been rather cross with him lately for coming home late in the evenings. The tailor thought, 'What a nice present it would make for her! And she will surely forgive me for coming home late so often!'

So he said to the rat, 'This cloth is too good for you. You could easily sell it and make some money! In fact, I am willing to give you a good price for it. Why do you want to waste it on a shirt for yourself?'

'I am going to meet the princess, that is why!' announced the rat grandly.

The tailor opened his eyes wide, pretending to be impressed and said, 'Hmm! And perhaps she's going to marry you?'

'Perhaps!' replied the rat. 'Hurry up, please! Will you or won't you make a shirt for me?' he asked.

'Sure thing! Anything for the royal bridegroom!' replied the tailor sarcastically and took the cloth from the rat.

But the cloth was so soft and silky that, as the tailor started to cut, it slipped from under his fingers and it got cut all wrong.

'Oh no! You've messed up everything! Now how will I ever get my nice shirt? Either give me back my cloth as it was or else give me that pearl ring!' demanded the rat. He squeaked and scampered about the tailor's house baring his sharp teeth.

Now, the tailor had with him cloth from many of his customers waiting to be stitched. He did not want the rat to gnaw at his customers' fabrics with his sharp teeth. 'I'll lose my livelihood if my regular customers go to another tailor!' he thought. So he agreed to give the rat the pearl ring, wondering about the excuses he would have to cook up for his wife to explain the loss of her ring.

The rat quickly grabbed the ring and ran on in the direction of the palace. 'Shirt or no shirt, I must get to see the princess!' he said to himself.

At the palace he slipped past the door man, the courtiers and all the king's ministers with ease. 'So, no one bothers about an insignificant rat!' he thought. 'Just you all wait and see!'

So saying the rat went right up to the king's throne. Now, the king was a rather huge man. To the rat he looked simply gigantic! Like the door-man, the courtiers and the ministers, the king did not notice the rat either. 'Just because you tower over me, you think you can ignore me completely! I'll teach you all a lesson!' thought the rat.

The rat gnawed lightly at the king's feet to get his attention. The king was so startled that he screamed and jumped off the throne and fell down. His leg knocked the rat, but being a frisky fellow, the rat quickly gathered himself up and climbed on to the hand rest of the king's throne. The king was on the floor and the rat on the throne! The rat bowed to the king from there and said, 'Your majesty! I do hope you are not hurt! But I hope even more that my pearl ring has not been damaged in this melee! I have come all the way to show it to you — it is a very special magic pearl ring!'

The courtiers picked up the king and helped him to the throne once more. The king dusted himself and looked around. He saw that the rat was talking to him from the throne's hand rest. 'What magic pearl ring?' asked the king.

'How can a mere rat have a pearl ring, magic or otherwise?' remarked a minister.

'He's probably making it up just to get attention!' remarked another.

'I am not making it up! It must have fallen here somewhere! Your Highness probably fell on it! Sir, will you please ask for a search to be made?' requested the rat.

The king was intrigued. He ordered a search at once. In no time at all the ring was found. But the pearl had fallen off and the gold was bent out of shape!

'Oh, no!' wailed the rat. 'It won't be magic any more!'

'It was my fault!' confessed the kind-hearted king. 'I was startled by your voice, you see. So I must have fallen on the ring! I am truly sorry! Ask for something, I'd like to compensate you in some way.'

Now, in actual fact, the ring had no magic powers. The rat had bluffed on that point. But he had wanted to make the most of the situation. So, pressing his advantage, he demanded, 'Either give me back my ring as it was with its magic powers or give me your daughter in marriage! I will accept no less!'

That is how the rat ended up marrying the princess. Do you wonder that the rat's favourite rhyme was:

Even though insignificant,
No money, no home, nor dress;
Use your wits, don't say I can't,
Aim high, marry a princess!

11

The Rat with a Hat

There once was a rat. One day, while rolling around in the mud he found a dirty rag.

"What should I do with this rag?" the rat wondered. "Hmm! May be I'll get a hat stitched. But first I must get this rag washed clean."

So the rat went to Dhobi, the washerman. "Dhobi Dada! O Dhobi Dada! Will you please wash my rag for me?"

Dhobi replied, "Get lost you dirty rat! I don't wash for the likes of you!"

"Is that so?" demanded the rat. And he announced in a sing-song voice:

> "I'll go to the chavadi then
> Get hold of four policemen.
> What fun to watch the lot of them
> Beat you up till the count of ten!"

Now the washerman did not want any unnecessary trouble. "Oh no, please don't!" he replied. "I'll wash your rag for you!"

So the rat got his rag washed. It became so clean and white that it no longer looked like a dirty rag.

Next the rat took his bit of white cloth and went to Rangari, the dyer. "Rangari Dada! O Rangari Dada! Will you please dye my cloth for me? I'd like a bright red!

Rangari the dyer replied, "Get lost you dirty rat! I don't dye for the likes of you!"

"Is that so?" demanded the rat. And he announced in a sing-song voice:

> "I'll go to the chavadi then
> Get hold of four policemen
> What fun to watch the lot of them
> Beat you up till the count of ten!"

Like Dhobi, Rangari wanted no trouble with policemen. "Oh no, please don't!" he replied. "I'll dye your cloth for you! It will be a nice red."

So the rat got his white cloth dyed. It became a bright red, just the way he wanted it to be.

Then the rat went to Shimpi, the tailor.

"Shimpi Dada! O Shimpi Dada! Will you please make a hat for me with this nice red cloth?"

Shimpi the tailor replied, "Get lost you dirty rat! I don't stitch for the likes of you!"

"Is that so?" demanded the rat. And he announced in a sing-song voice:

"I'll go to the chavadi then
Get hold of four policemen
What fun to watch the lot of them
Beat you up till the count of ten!"

Like Dhobi and Rangari, Shimpi too wanted no trouble with policemen. "Oh no, please don't!" he replied. "I'll take your cloth and stitch a smart hat for you."

So the rat got his cloth made into a smart, red hat, just the way he wanted.

"Wouldn't it be nice if it were decorated with some tassels and zari?" wondered the rat. So the rat went to Gondya-zari Bai, the woman who embroidered and did some fine zari, bead and tassel work.

"Gondya-zari Bai, O Gondya-zari Bai! Will you please decorate my red hat with some tassels and zari? I want a really fancy hat!"

Gondya-zari Bai replied, "Get lost you dirty rat! I don't decorate for the likes of you!"

"Is that so?" demanded the rat. And he announced in a sing-song voice:

"I'll go to the chavadi then
Get hold of four policemen
What fun to watch the lot of them
Beat you up till the count of ten!"

Just like Dhobi, Rangari and Shimpi, Gondya-zari Bai too wanted no trouble with policemen. "Oh no, please don't!" she replied. "I'll take your red hat and decorate it with some yellow tassels and golden zari."

So the rat got his red hat decorated. Now it looked really grand. How pleased the rat was with his new hat! He wore it and strutted about on the main street in town pretending to be a king.

The king was actually passing by with some of his courtiers at that time. One of them saw the tiny creature preening right in the middle of the road. He picked up the rat in his hand to get a better look. How surprised he was! He took the rat-with-a-hat to the king saying, "Sir, here is something that might delight you!"

The king placed the rat-with-a-hat on the palm of his hand to take a good look. He pulled the hat off the rat's head, then set the rat down and turned the little hat around in his hand. The rat was annoyed to be separated from his hat. He started singing:

> "The king is a pauper, did you all know that?
> Why else would he take away my hat?"

People on the street stared. The king was stung. "Give back the hat to that silly rat!" he ordered, flinging the hat down. The rat started off his singing again:

> "The king is scared, did you all know that?
> Why else would he return my hat?"

Totally frustrated, the king and his courtiers went away, outsmarted by a tiny rat-with-a-hat.

12

The Tired Storyteller

The children had been listening to stories all evening. The storyteller was tired. Her jaws began to ache. Her throat was sore. She wanted to go home for rest and food. But the listeners wanted more. All the children pleaded.

"Please, just one more!" begged one.

"We won't trouble you after that!" said another.

"We all promise!" said a third.

"Do you all really and truly promise?" asked the storyteller.

"Yes, we do!" shouted everyone in chorus.

"Very well, then! But this will be the last story for today!" declared the storyteller.

"We agree!" said the children.

"All right! Let me think," said the tired storyteller, closing her eyes and taking a deep breath.

This is what happened next.

Storyteller: Should I tell you the story of the cotton carder?

Children: Yes!

Storyteller: Yes? What do you mean by 'yes'? Should I tell you the story of the cotton carder?

Children: Yes, yes!

Storyteller: What is the meaning of 'yes, yes'? Should I tell you the story of the cotton carder?

Children: Yes, yes, of course!

Storyteller: Yes, yes, of course? What is 'yes, yes, of course'? Should I tell you the story of the cotton carder?

Children: Oh, come on! Hurry up!

Storyteller: Oh, come on! Hurry up! What do you mean by 'Oh, come on! Hurry up!'? Should I tell you the story of the cotton carder?

Children: That's not fair! You're not telling us any story!

Storyteller: That's not fair! You're not telling us any story? What is 'That's not fair! You're not telling us any story'? Should I tell you the story of the cotton carder?

This went on for a while. Finally the children had had enough. Then this is what happened.

Children: Okay, okay! Forget it!

Storyteller: Okay, okay! Forget it! What do you mean, 'Okay, okay! Forget it!'? Should I tell you the story of the cotton carder?

Children: No, please! We give up!

Storyteller: No, please! We give up! Why do you say, 'No, please! We give up!'? Should I tell you the story of the cotton carder?

Children: Please! We've had enough! We just want to go home!

Storyteller: Oh, all right! If you all insist! Good night everyone!